BAD APPLE

For Nelly.
A perfect pip.
HUW

For Juelz.
The apple of my eye.
BEN

BAD APPLE

HUW LEWIS JONES
& BEN SANDERS

This is Apple.

He's a nasty
piece of fruit.

Just you wait.

Apple and Pear.

Life's not fair.
It was Pear's chair.

Apple and Pea.

Oh, dearie me.
He drank Pea's tea.

Apple and Cat.

Now fancy that.
He stole Cat's hat.

Apple and Spud.

With one big thud,
pushed in the mud.

He spoiled Spoon's tune.

He broke Egg's leg.

He pinched Peach and Plum,
and then Plum's mum!

Apple and Orange.

Well, that was
never going to work.

Apple and Rose.

Guess how it goes...

He stood on his toes
to pull Rose's nose.

Apple and Pie.

Told a lie
that made him cry.
Then poked Pie's eye!

Such a bad apple.

Apple and Snake
begin to bake.

But what a mistake...

...to eat Snake's cake.

Best not be rude
when you're just food.

Oh bother.

Huw Lewis Jones is a polar-exploring author and historian who lives in Cornwall, UK. His books include *Explorers' Sketchbooks*, *The Writer's Map* and *Archipelago* (all Thames & Hudson).

Ben Sanders is an award-winning illustrator and graphic designer based in Ballarat, Australia. He is the author and illustrator of *I've an Uncle Ivan* and *I Could Wear That Hat!* (both Thames & Hudson Australia).

First published in the United Kingdom in 2021 by
Thames & Hudson Ltd, 181A High Holborn, London WC1V 7QX

Bad Apple © 2021 Thames & Hudson Ltd, London

Concept and Text © 2021 Huw Lewis Jones
Illustration and Design © 2021 Ben Sanders

British Library Cataloguing-in-Publication Data
A catalogue record for this book is available from the British Library

ISBN 978-0-500-65243-5

Printed in China by Shanghai Offset Printing Products Limited

Be the first to know about our new releases,
exclusive content and author events by visiting
thamesandhudson.com
thamesandhudsonusa.com
thamesandhudson.com.au